Dear Parents:

Congratulations! Your child is taking the first steps on an exciting journey. The destination? Independent reading!

STEP INTO READING® will help your child get there. The program offers five steps to reading success. Each step includes fun stories and colorful art or photographs. In addition to original fiction and books with favorite characters, there are Step into Reading Non-Fiction Readers, Phonics Readers and Boxed Sets, Sticker Readers, and Comic Readers—a complete literacy program with something to interest every child.

Learning to Read, Step by Step!

Ready to Read   Preschool–Kindergarten
• big type and easy words • rhyme and rhythm • picture clues
For children who know the alphabet and are eager to begin reading.

Reading with Help   Preschool–Grade 1
• basic vocabulary • short sentences • simple stories
For children who recognize familiar words and sound out new words with help.

Reading on Your Own   Grades 1–3
• engaging characters • easy-to-follow plots • popular topics
For children who are ready to read on their own.

Reading Paragraphs   Grades 2–3
• challenging vocabulary • short paragraphs • exciting stories
For newly independent readers who read simple sentences with confidence.

Ready for Chapters   Grades 2–4
• chapters • longer paragraphs • full-color art
For children who want to take the plunge into chapter books but still like colorful pictures.

STEP INTO READING® is designed to give every child a successful reading experience. The grade levels are only guides; children will progress through the steps at their own speed, developing confidence in their reading.

Remember, a lifetime love of reading starts with a single step!

For my brother, Kevin
—C.B.C.

WWW.JURASSICPARK.COM
Jurassic World is a trademark and copyright of Universal Studios and Amblin Entertainment, Inc. Licensed by Universal Studios Licensing LLC. All Rights Reserved.

© 2015 by Universal Studios and Amblin Entertainment, Inc. Published in the United States by Random House Children's Books, a division of Penguin Random House LLC, 1745 Broadway, New York, NY 10019, and in Canada by Random House of Canada, a division of Penguin Random House Ltd., Toronto. Step into Reading, Random House, and the Random House colophon are registered trademarks of Penguin Random House LLC.

Visit us on the Web!
StepIntoReading.com
randomhousekids.com

Educators and librarians, for a variety of teaching tools, visit us at RHTeachersLibrarians.com

ISBN 978-0-553-53687-4 (trade) — ISBN 978-0-553-53688-1 (lib. bdg.) — ISBN 978-0-553-53689-8 (ebook)

Printed in the United States of America
10 9 8 7 6 5 4 3 2 1

DANGER: DINOSAURS!

Adapted by Courtney Carbone

Random House 🏠 New York

Millions of years ago,
dinosaurs and other
prehistoric creatures
ruled the land,
the oceans,
and the open sky.

Jurassic World brings to life
the most dangerous creatures
ever to stalk the earth.

Triceratops

(trie-SAIR-a-tops)

The word Triceratops means
"three-horned face."
These were the largest
of the horned dinosaurs,
weighing up to ten tons!

Baby Triceratops hatched
out of melon-sized eggs.
They grew into their horns:
one over the nose
and two over the eyes.

Triceratops had a large,

solid frill on their head

to protect against predators.

This probably came in handy!
Many experts believe
Triceratops fought with
the Tyrannosaurus rex!

Apatosaurus

(a-PAT-o-SAWR-us)

The Apatosaurus was
one of the largest animals
ever to walk the earth.
A grown Apatosaurus was
longer than two school buses!

The Apatosaurus mostly ate
ferns and conifer branches.
Because it could not chew,
it had to swallow all
of its food whole!

Stegosaurus

(STEG-o-SAWR-us)

The Stegosaurus had 17 broad plates running down its neck and back. These plates could grow up to 30 inches long!

Stegosaurus had a tail
with four long spikes.
If threatened by a predator,
this herbivore could swing
its tail for defense.

Ankylosaurus

(ANG-ki-lo-SAWR-us)

The word Ankylosaurus means "fused lizard." This massive dinosaur weighed up to six tons!

Luckily for other dinosaurs,
Ankylosaurus lived on a diet
of ferns and other plants.

Scientists sometimes call Ankylosaurus a "living tank." This is because it was protected by spiky armor.

The armor ran all the
way from its skull to its tail.
An Ankylosaurus's tail was
shaped like a giant club.

Gallimimus

(GAL-i-MIME-us)

Gallimimus is sometimes called the "chicken mimic." But this birdlike dinosaur weighed almost 500 pounds!

Like modern birds,
these reptiles may have
lived in flocks.
They could escape
predators by running
almost 30 miles per hour!

Velociraptor

(vuh-LOS-ih-RAP-tor)

Velociraptors were
fierce prehistoric predators.
These carnivores were
a dangerous threat
to many types of prey.

Velociraptors stood
on two feet like humans.
Experts believe that they
may have been one of the
smartest dinosaur species.

Velociraptors hunted in packs,
working together to weaken
and kill their unlucky prey.

These carnivores were
always ready to strike
with the razor-sharp
claws on each foot.

Tyrannosaurus

(tie-RAN-o-SAWR-us)

The name Tyrannosaurus
means "tyrant lizard."
The T. rex was one of the
most fearsome creatures
of all time.

The T. rex had a diet
of flesh and bone.
It ate up to 22 tons
of meat per year.

You have probably heard
that T. rexes had tiny arms.
But some experts believe
that their small arms were
actually very powerful.

T. rexes may have fought over meals and mates. Scientists have even found T. rex fossils with tooth marks from other T. rexes!

Dimorphodon

(die-MOR-fo-don)

Dimorphodons were flying reptiles.

They would glide over large bodies of water in search of fish to eat.

Pteranodon

(te-RAN-o-don)

The Pteranodon had
a huge wingspan!
This flying reptile used
a long, pointy beak
to catch and eat marine life.

Mosasaurus

(MO-za-SAWR-us)

Mosasaurus was a huge marine reptile that weighed 30,000 pounds and measured about 60 feet long.

Experts believe it was related to modern-day lizards and snakes. These prehistoric creatures were carnivores that ate fish and other sea creatures.

Which *Jurassic World* creature do you think is the most dangerous?